While the Horses Galloped to London

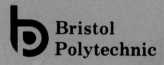
Bristol
Polytechnic

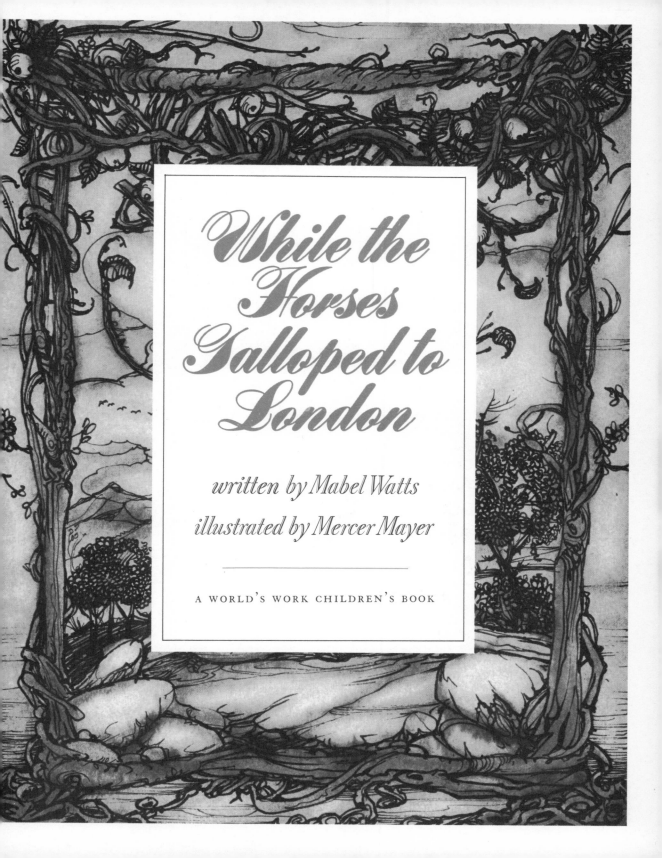

While the Horses Galloped to London

written by Mabel Watts

illustrated by Mercer Mayer

A WORLD'S WORK CHILDREN'S BOOK

Text copyright © 1973 by Mabel Watts
Illustrations copyright © 1973 by Mercer Mayer
All rights reserved

First published in Great Britain 1974 by
World's Work Ltd
The Windmill Press
Kingswood, Tadworth, Surrey

Printed in Great Britain by
William Clowes & Sons, Limited
London, Beccles and Colchester

SBN 437 84210 X

To Pat

It happened in England, many long years ago, when Sherman was nothing but a boy. At nine o'clock in the morning, a stagecoach with four galloping horses drew up before the village inn with a rattle, a rumble, and a clatter of hoofs.

"All aboard for London!" shouted the driver, as his horses rested. "Two shillings to London!"

One by one the passengers paid their fares and climbed aboard.

There was a woman carrying a bag of knitting.

A little girl cuddling a china-faced doll.

A fishwife carrying a basket of cockles and mussels.

A sailor home from the sea, with a parrot in a cage.

A singer with a yellow moustache and a fiddle.

There was a magician who wore a tall black hat with a rabbit inside it.

And Sherman was last.

He carried a stewpot that was to be a present for his grandmother in London.

"Watch out for robbers, outlaws and highwaymen," said his mother, "and guard that pot with your life!"

"Not for a king's ransom will I give it up to anyone," said Sherman. "So don't you worry."

"A pot that big belongs on top with the trunks and boxes," said the driver from his high-up seat.

"Not for one minute will I take my eyes off this pot," said Sherman, "for I must guard it with my life!"

"Then let it stay," said the driver. He cracked his whip over the horses' heads, and off they went at a breakneck speed.

For want of a better place to put the pot, Sherman held it tightly on his lap, while the horses galloped to London.

But it was too much pot for one lap.

"With your pot taking up most of *my* lap," said the lady with the knitting, "I have no room to knit!"

"With your pot sitting on *my* lap," said the singer with the yellow moustache, "I have no room to play my fiddle!"

To keep them from complaining, and for want of a better place to keep the pot, Sherman set it on a rack overhead, while the horses galloped to London.

All went merrily enough till the wheels bumped over a rut in the road. This jerked the pot off the rack and sent it tumbling down on the tall black hat below.

"Smashed to smithereens!" said the magician sadly. "And if my rabbit hadn't been safe in my pocket, things might have been worse!"

To keep the magician from complaining, and
for want of a better place to keep the pot,
Sherman set it on the floor by his feet, while the
horses galloped to London.

"With your pot on the floor, there's no room
for *my* feet," said the sailor home from the sea.
"And there's no room for my parrot in his cage."

"There's no room for my basket full of cockles and mussels," said the fishwife.

To keep the sailor and the fishwife from complaining, and for want of a better place to keep the pot, Sherman gave up his seat to the pot. He stood at the window, while the horses galloped to London.

"Now my pot won't bother anyone," said Sherman, "because it's sitting in the seat that is rightfully mine—the seat for which my mother paid a two-shilling fare!"

But putting the pot on his seat did not mend matters.

"With you standing in the window, my china-faced
doll can't see the scenery," said the little girl. "She can't
see the flowers in the dingles, or the dragons in the dells,
and all because your silly pot has to have a seat!"

"That pot is a nuisance!" said the passengers. "That
boy is a pest!"

"Quiet down there," shouted the driver. "You're upsetting the horses!"

To keep *everyone* from complaining, Sherman wondered if he shouldn't get off the coach and walk the rest of the way to London.

But just as he was making up his mind...an outlaw saved him the trouble.

It was Rough Roger himself, on his fiery white stallion, and he was fiery as a hornet.

"Your money or your life!" he said, bold as brass, as the four galloping horses came to a stop. "And remember, I am the wildest, the wickedest highwayman in all of England!"

At the sight of his gun, the passengers got off the coach
and dropped their money into Rough Roger's hat—
sovereigns, guineas, and silver crowns—every last farthing,
from every last pocket.

"Hand over your valuables as well," said Rough Roger.
"And remember, you'll be sorry if you try to trick me!"

The knitting-lady gave up her knitting.

The fishwife gave up her basket of cockles and mussels.

The sailor gave up his parrot, cage and all.

The singer with the yellow moustache gave up his fiddle.

With a tear in her eye, the little girl gave up her china-faced doll.

The magician gave up his rabbit and all that was left of the tall black hat.

But Sherman would not give up his pot. "It's a present for my grandmother in London," he said, "and I will guard it with my life!"

He planted himself fair and square before Rough Roger. "Not for a king's ransom will I give up this pot," he said. "Anyway, it has a hole..."

"A hole, you say," said Rough Roger, and he peered into the pot, thinking what a fine stew he would make of the rabbit. "I don't see a hole!"

"Look a little closer," said Sherman bravely, though he was nothing but a boy, and his heart was beating like a bird in a hand.

Rough Roger looked closer. "If there's a hole in this pot," he said, "I must be needing some spectacles!"

But just as he said, "spectacles," Sherman pushed the outlaw's head all the way into the pot, and it was a very tight fit. It fitted him so tightly he couldn't pull it off.

"If there *hadn't* been a hole in this pot," Sherman told Rough Roger, "you couldn't have got your head inside!"

"That's a good joke for a boy your size," said the magician, as he took back his rabbit and all that was left of his tall black hat.

"Your pot was just the right size for catching an outlaw,"

said the sailor, home from the sea, as he comforted the
parrot in the cage.

"At a time like this there was no better place to put the
pot," said the little girl as she cuddled her china-faced doll.

"No other boy would have had the courage to outwit
Rough Roger," everyone said. "The wildest,
the wickedest outlaw in all of England!"

They laughed all the way to the jail in the next
town, where it took three blacksmiths and a team of
horses to pull the pot off Rough Roger's head.

After that, Sherman had no more trouble at all with his pot. Everyone was proud to hold it.

"Your pot is *not* a nuisance," they said. "And you are anything but a pest!"

"Wait till my grandmother hears about *this*," said Sherman.

While the horses galloped to London.

THE END